Intangible Boundaries

POETIC GESTURES OF LIFE

Todd McManus

Order this book online at www.trafford.com
or email orders@trafford.com

Most Trafford titles are also available at major online book retailers.

Note for Librarians: A cataloguing record for this book is available from Library
and Archives Canada at www.collectionscanada.ca/amicus/index-e.html

Printed in Victoria, BC, Canada.

ISBN: 978-1-4269-1697-7

Library of Congress Control Number: 2009936631

*Our mission is to efficiently provide the world's finest, most
comprehensive book publishing service, enabling every author to
experience success. To find out how to publish your book, your way, and
have it available worldwide, visit us online at www.trafford.com*

Trafford rev. 10/22/2009

Trafford
PUBLISHING® www.trafford.com

North America & international
toll-free: 1 888 232 4444 (USA & Canada)
phone: 250 383 6864 • fax: 812 355 4082

Dedicated to the woman
who inspired me to complete
this book. Your presence in my
life has been a welcoming flame.
To God for the gift of expression
and my precious daughters,
Aniah & Tatyana.

What You Want

Just because I think of you
Doesn't mean I want you
Even though you play with me
Doesn't mean we have to be
You like it when I come around
But this is nothing new you've found
You flirt to see if I will break
And wonder just which road I'll take
You act as if there's something there
Or even if I really care
You like the game and love the chase
I play along, but just in case
This turns to more than just your joke
Don't try to break what's already broke
If you saw me as I see you
You wouldn't wonder as you do
You're trying to figure me out but don't
Just tell me what it is you want

Baby Boy

What a gift the Lord has made
A beautiful baby a precious trade
But not the life of mine
Pretending in places to save your face
Of a shameful heartfelt disgrace
That would play itself out in time

My belief in you is what you flaunted
A chance for us you never wanted
Only to draw me nearer
I tried to accept the words you said
My heart spoke yes but not my head
And now I see you clearer

You only needed me when you needed him
Your glow for me grew quite dim
While constantly I thought, maybe
Maybe this could work its no one's fault
Just another lesson that time has taught
But wait, you're still having a baby

"I have to be careful, no I must be smart"
Only God knows what's in my heart
But for yours I was unsure
Convincing myself I was wrong to be mad
Listening carefully as you spoke of his dad
I saw your heart of me unpure

What a sad way for us to end
You'd become my true best friend
Such a very close-knit pair
Making me believe your affair was a game
Your baby boy you gave his name
Seemingly so unfair

What insight to keep my distance
Protecting my heart against its resistance
Still the dagger pierced my soul
Blood of betrayal poured out onto the floor
Deceitful pain is the scar I wore
As the true you took its toll
… damn

Born of Beauty

Her eyes are eyes of love and passion
Her clothes are of the finest fashion

Her lips speak words so sweet and kind
Her face is smooth and oh so fine

Her looks are sexy as can be
I want this one to be with me

Her hands are soft with warmth to give
for this lady my life I'd live

Her sweet embrace is nicely tender
and by her asking I will surrender

By hearing her voice I am impressed
I know this one was truly blessed

She is one I'd hate to miss
her lovely lips I aim to kiss

For this lady I care so much
so deeply fragile is her touch

A lady like this is what I need
and the one I want is you indeed

Blind Hearts

Why do you lead when you cannot see
You're only out to embarrass me
I say dumb things I really can't mean
While telling myself it's honesty

I try not to listen to what you say
You make me weak from day to day
I close my ears, I hide my fears
But somehow you still get your way

Stop making me feel on top of the world
You know I only just met this girl
You race, I pace all over the place
But that only makes my head swirl

Why do you make me care so fast
Knowing if rushed it will not last
Relax sometime so I can use my mind
Why can't you learn from the past

Stop making me feel all crazy inside
These nervous feelings I cannot hide
You need to hush, besides what's the rush
Every girl we meet can't be our bride

Black Frost

Ah yeah, its that time again boys & girls
time for treats, goodies, and gifts.
but don't be taken by the hype
of the white man's Christmas myth

You see, mom & dad worked real hard
sometimes all night and all day
just to be sure you are not without
on this happy holiday

They may not give all that you want
but it will be all that they can
because they are the ones who love you
not some big fat ho-ho'ing white man

So always remember boys & girls
your parents deserve the credit
their blessings from God they give to you
and don't you ever forget it

Black I Stand

Black I come time after time
to make them understand
I only want acceptance that's due
acceptance of a *free* Black man

Coming Black is always a struggle
I am seen but never heard
my Black skin speaks so loud
they never hear a word

I warned you all of self-destruction
consequences of death I'd tell
but because I came as Moses
you chose to go to hell

I asked for freedom to live in peace
we have suffered and cried many tears
but because I came as Mandela
I was jailed for 27 years

When ready to stand up I sat down
in the first available space
but because I came as Rosa
you wanted me to stay in my place

I showed you love in spite of your hate
my mission was not a loss
but because I came as Jesus
you hung me on a cross

I demanded the rights you promised me
with a tongue as sharp as a knife
but because I came as Malcolm
you plotted to end my life

I asked to be treated with decency
as a man and not a slave
but because I came as Martin
my freedom came in a grave

Now here I stand young, gifted, and Black
ready, deserving, and willing
but because I don't fit your profile
I'm stopped by your glass ceiling

You whipped, you hosed, you labeled me
you said I was 3/5 of a man
you harass, you murder, you incarcerate me
but still day-by-day I'll stand

Blue Funk

A funk that's bold
A funk that's new
A funk that's felt
A funk that's true
A funk that's hard
And overdue
A funk that's cold
A funk that's blue
A funk that burns
And sticks like glue
A funk that's real
A funk that's you
A funk that's sad
Where loneliness grew
A funk of tears
A funk like stew
A funk that clouds
Your point of view
A funk of poison
A funk that's blue

Bubbles In The Night

From a light sleep
to a soaring roar
the bubbles begin to flow
with eyes barely closed
I could scream til I'm blue
and she would never know

In a sleep so deep
she'll never wake up
but I can hear she's not dead
I try shaking her
but that doesn't work
just bubbles floating from my bed

"Bubble, bubble
toil and trouble"
what am I going to do
It seems as though
she's looking at me
but I guess that just ain't true

If I leave her there
fast asleep
she'll be out all night
and I'll run the risk
of waking up
in a bubble when comes daylight

Call On Me

When life to you
seems so unfair
and friends you knew
seem not to care
call me

When money is short
and bills are due
when no one comes
to your rescue
call me

When things go wrong
and you can't win
you want to quit
but don't give in
call me

When you try hard
to give your best
when confusion causes
weary unrest
call me

Call my name
and I'll be there
for I am he
who will always care
so when the pressures
of life increase
forever I'm here
to bring you peace
call me, Jesus

Choices

I stayed because I believed in you
your love captured my soul
so many dreams I had for us
will now go left untold

Ready to share my life with you
but you had other plans
so now the love I felt was true
is no longer in demand

I allowed you to take control of me
to use me as you would
facing ups & downs, yes, maybe, no
realizing we're through for good

Hearing your voice excited me
when talking on the phone
now hearing you in suspicion
I want to be left alone

I must find myself again
take control of my own life
letting no one get this close to me
not a friend, lover, or wife

I came to the place my life began
not knowing what I'd do
I thought my love would grasp your heart
seems I was just passing through

My heart tells me my life's gone wrong
and there's nothing left to say
I came to you to fulfill my life
but you chose to send me away

Confusion

Wondering what is to come
from what we have
yet not knowing if we have
or even if it's worth the time
to go through changes

being together yet so alone
feeling unanswered and wondering
wondering still what will be
of what is not
and how that came to be

thus confusion in one's mind
is said to be
an eclipse of love
in the shadow of hearts
destined for eternity -never to be set free

Day Dream

The smell of your sweet body
while away from you
still runs fresh through my mind
the warmth, the softness
of your beautiful skin
moving forward only to rewind

The fast pace of my heart
when I lay next to you
never wanting the feeling to end
the taste of your neck
while wanting much more
even though you are my friend

The kiss from your sexy lips
that I keep dreaming of
still escalates my emotion
the touch of your ecstasy
your voice in my head
like tender love and devotion

The look in your lovely eyes
while talking with you
entangled with the way you feel
he didn't treat you
like the woman you are
but believe in me, I will

I Am Love

Quit playing you know me,
then again you don't
I try to get close to you ,
but close to me you won't
When you look at me what you see is me
a man, a mortal, or maybe a messiah
But you never see me
cause I'm at a level much higher
Yeah higher than your mind
and much deeper than your heart
I'm the one who stood by you even from the start
But all you ever noticed were lies and deceit
from them niggas in the street
He would kiss you and then hit you
And you believed that that was me,
but it's not
For I am love

You once thought you knew me,
but we've never even met
You gave up sex for a bet
but that's the closest you could get to me
Saying "I Love You" 'cause you're dating or
just because you're going steady
When you really should be waiting
'cause the truth is you're not ready
For the bullshit he will feed you
while he tells you that he needs you
but he don't know how to please you
but tease you when he sees you
Pumping faster and faster thinking that he
has to to win you
Until he bust one and then asks you if you
feel me, but you don't
For I am love

Ordinary? No, extraordinary. I'm not an
ordinary love.
Like just saying I Love You 'cause the mood
is right
Or he's there all night trying to get a bite or
trying to see if you might
But I'm an emotion of uncontrollable desire
that sets your soul on fire
My level of sensation is too much to admire
For I am the one, the only truth you should aspire
I am love

Dead Blue

Thoughts of laughter while reminded of you
are never too hard to find
filled with smiles, but still I'm blue
for they exist only in my mind

I try moving on, but what can I do
meeting others everyday
those times are fun, but still I'm blue
ever since you went away

We shared a love that was so true
or at least that's how it seemed
how happy we were, but still I'm blue
for your love was not redeemed

So now you're happy with someone new
and I have a special friend
I want much more, but still I'm blue
for our dream came to an end

There are so many things we've been through
things we sometimes regret
those times have passed, but still I'm blue
for it's you I can't forget

Seems I was lost without a clue
but things would change I knew
so here I am alone and blue
and it's all for loving you

Deliver Me

Deliver me oh Lord I pray
remove the pain and sorrow
help us to understand "it's now"
for good-byes may come tomorrow

Help us to live and grow in you
for the world is filled with tears
tears that never go away
tears of all our fears

And now the time has come for me
to put away the hurt
to leave this place and enter one
from which I came, the earth

So dry the eyes of family & friends
this decision I have made
there were no words to be said by any
the result I would not trade

Protect the woman I love so much
keep her happy and filled with love
and though I'm not there to harden her heart
I'll look down from up above

See, life for me seemed much to bear
in every direction I'd fall
now I know that living my life
isn't really living at all

So here I am today, oh Lord
with one request of thee
take my soul and make me whole
please Lord, deliver me

Do I Do What I Do

Did I think to myself that I am not myself
and my thoughts are not my own
And am I hearing others tell me what to think
or is this something I should have known

Did I do what I did because I wanted
or was it something I heard someone say
And am I with the person I want to be with
or is this someone that was pushed my way

Did I decide on my action because it pleases me
or was it something I was told to do
And am I really the person I say I am
or are these words I have heard too

Did I say what I said because it was what I meant
or was I coached on how to feel at the time
And am I "wishy-washy" because I'm not sure
or because others keep changing my mind

Did I leave because it was best for me
or because someone said I should go
And if I decided it all for myself
will others believe it was so

Did I allow myself to get like this
or is this how I was told to be
And if I continue to live this way
how can I ever be me

Abstract Fantasy

Sweet dreams of her yet deep inside
never to leave his mind
such dreams of man to wish then hide
in a place no other can find

With unexpected emotions of joy
each time he hears her name
while being a man, yet still a boy
playing life as if a game

To touch her even though she's not there
realizing she'll never be
does she think of him or even care
how abstract the reality

Up above the snow white clouds
beyond the life of death
within the hearts of unborn crowds
never to share his wealth

He looks into his future's past
hoping to find forever
but even if found it would not last
for fantasy comes only never

Find the Words

I know you've had the life I seek
the marriage, the child, the love
but for some reason unknown to me
you want this life no more

In you I see a woman so true
there's love and then there's pain
now unsure of what to do
with me yet alone the same

How can I tell you just how I feel
will you ever understand
life for me has been unreal
but still I reach out my hand

I call your name even in my sleep
I've waited for you so long
around you all I do is think
and pray nothing goes wrong

How can one lady mean so much
in such a very short time
my heart melts just from the touch
of your hand or face near mine

You pull away saying it's too soon
you want to be fair, you say
I only dream of being your groom
if ever I see the day

There's so much love I want to give
if only I could find the words
to make you believe for you I'd live
if I only could find the words

Fragile Possibilities

Could it be that we should meet
Only for a while
Or are you just a memory
For me to reconcile

Are we to remain only as friends
Without ever knowing the extent
Or are you just a representation
Of a time I was content

Could it be that you are here
To show me love again
Or are you just a heavenly angel
Sent to hold my hand

Is there a chance that you and I
Were meant to be together
Or is the spark I feel inside
A sign of changing weather

Did you feel when our lips met
A burning within your soul
Or do you enjoy coming near me
To exercise your level of control

Could it be that what we share
Can really begin to grow
Or does exploring the possibilities
Scare you into saying no

Love Of A Friend

Friends we are and always will be
but hidden feelings are part of me

These unknown feelings I can't explain
I try to let go, yet they remain

They're so confusing -so abstract
and yet so real I can't react

It seems no matter what I do
I'm possessed by thoughts of you

I found in you a real true friend
on me forever you can depend

Your pretty brown eyes let me know you care
just call on me and I'll be there

To me you're so helpful, so kind, so sweet
a friendship like ours cannot be beat

A listener to problems, you took the time
for every penny thought you've earned a dime

what's so special about you I just can't place
it could be your kindness, your love, your face

We both have hurt feelings from others we hide
but now in each other we can confide

It seems so hard waiting for pain to end
but I thank God for love of a friend

Frustrations of Love

I try to persuade you
but what's the use
you'll never have me I know
with all my heart
I feel the abuse
of hearing that I must go

I want to tell you
that I was wrong
a grand mistake I've made
you'll never be hurt
or even alone
my love will never fade

It's very hard
admitting I've lost
not knowing how things will be
will it make a difference
that I'm paying the cost
while you're away from me

There's so much tension
between us two
but things will get better I pray
I've been a fool
now what do I do
are there any right words to say

Scars of rejection
that lay on my heart
continue to follow my lead
missing you daily
while we're apart
leaves an unfilled need

I want to touch you
to show I care
with blessings from up above
when you needed me
I was not there
replaced by frustrations of love

Hocus Pocus

Unleash this spell that covers me
I don't know her at all
What kind of magic does she possess
Pushing my heart against the wall

Maybe it was her controlling eyes
That made me feel so drawn to her
Or maybe just her lovely smile
Is something I prefer

I never believed in love at first sight
But apparently it must be true
I must regain control of myself
To relinquish this feeling of blue

How carelessly I give in to her
As if I'm not really me
Lingering in a state of confusion
Break the spell and set me free

Lady

Like an angel from the heavens
her spirit follows my path
I can feel her around me
carefully watching

Looking to see if I'm sincere
can I be all that others believe
she listens to every word
wondering if I'm for real

I can smell her sweetness
like a bed of roses
she's beautifully filled with love
and constantly on my mind

She could come to me easily
and I would fall for her
she could be my reason
yeah, a true reason

She could look to me
and I would be her answer
we would be a union
one love, one life

Where are you Lady
what are your thoughts
are you somewhere lonely
how long will it take

My arms are opened wide
take the key to my heart
and come inside where you belong
take a chance, I'll be waiting

Liar of Love

Don't tell me you love me
if love is a lie
Don't tell me you miss me
if that makes you cry
Don't think of our future
if we have no past
Don't say that you're interested
if it cannot last
Don't tell me of another
if you just left me
Don't tell me you like him
for how can that be
Don't ask me to write you
if you do not care
Don't ask me to call you
if you are not there
Don't tell what I meant
if anything at all
Don't tell me you're sorry
if you're having a ball
Don't tell me it's over
if there was no beginning
Don't tell me "in time"
if you're starting our ending
Don't put me through heartache
if there is no cure
And don't tell me you love me
if love is not pure

Living

How can life really be this way
Bad most of the time and only good for a day
Falling in love to marry until death
But nothing seems to last as long as your health

A million times you play the song
But somehow it all goes wrong
Everything you are is still not enough
The downs of life makes it too tough

Everyone has such perfect dreams
But reality throws in so many things
You live each day with your head above water
While your only sign of strength comes from
your daughter

How can you live a life that's numb
From that what good can you become
In this situation you will never win
The past will beat you again and again

Find a way to end it all
Rise in spite of it rather than fall
It's never easy doing what's right
You only get one chance to live your life

Live it.

Lord Of Lords

On that great day
there was born a King
one with power unknown
with his kindness
he gave many things
and the wonders of his goodness was shown

He came to spread
his special love
though it would cost his life
a gift sent down
from heaven above
to relieve our grief and strife

But we knew not
how great a man
the Messiah would be to us
his spirit still felt
throughout the land
his grace we can always trust

It carries us on
from day to day
with blessings that overflow
his goodness and mercy
leads the way
causing our faith to grow

Oh Lord, our Lord
we honor thee
giving all thanks and praise
we glorify your name, you see
for bringing us through many days

Forgive us for
our many sins
even though we are to blame
and when ours lives
come to an end
please save us in your name. Amen.

Motion Sickness

Over and over
minute by minute
the same routine of life
over and over
hour after hour
a date but not a wife

Over and over
day by day
movies, dinners, and parks
over and over
week after week
chasing after the sparks

Over and over
month by month
more of myself I give
over and over
year after year
without a life I live

Over and over
season by season
I give up on the notion
over and over
time after time
sick of going through the motion

My Sister My Ass

If nothing is what you wanted
Saying nothing would have been easy
Instead pretending there was an interest
Was only your way to tease me
This feeling will pass
My sister, my ass

If little is what I meant to you
Little attention you should have given
Instead making me feel so special
Was where you wanted me driven
This feeling will pass
My sister, my ass

If friend is what I am to you
Friends we should have started
Instead full steam ahead to a love affair
You felt it was time you departed
This feeling will pass
My sister, my ass

If a brother is who I am like
Then my sister you should have been
Instead filling me up to let me down
Was only a game, did you win
This feeling must pass
My sister, my ass

She's In My Past

She calls because she misses me
She calls because she's lonely
She's trying to disrupt my life with you
hoping she'll be my one and only

I tried to have a life with her
I gave all that my heart would allow
I even asked her hand in marriage
but that was too sacred a vow

I gave up because it had been too long
trying hard to make things fit
She could never be all I needed
seems I was just digging my pit

When I noticed you all over again
I had to make it known
You were too cute, too nice, too warm to me
and I was on my own

I let you know what I thought of you
and you thought it was just a line
I never imagined the day would come
that I could call you mine

You make me feel so good inside
like a little kid at play
You're always on my mind it seems
and I love feeling this way

I know you're worried about the past
thinking there's more behind the scenes
But I could never hurt *us* that way
not even in my dreams

You have become a part of me
a part worth holding onto
Please don't judge me by what you think
judge me by what I do

I am a very honest person
any questions you have just ask
Ready or not the truth will come forth
I have no reason to wear a mask

I hope this places your mind at ease
our relationship I want to last
Do not allow this to get to you
please believe it...she's in my past

Reincarnation

Ever heard of reincarnation? Not like an
eradication called emancipation only after
dying to build a nation. Naw, that's too much
frustration. I'm talking about reincarnation.

Reincarnation. Not like when you die you
come back a fly with your head held high
watching your loved ones from the sky. And
no matter how you try you can't figure out
why when all you ever was was fly. But that's
not what I'm talking about.

I'm talking about reincarnation. Like life after
death, but in the same form even if you don't
know him. He's the one that calms the storm,
enlightens minds to recite poems, opening
university dorms to Black youths in swarms.
Not only should you know him, but adore
him.

I'm not talking about the reincarnation of
a race one by one that white America will
shun. Can't you see what they've done. Now
their kids have begun hurting each other
with guns. Sickly, they're the ones killing for
fun, but let me take you deeper, son.

Reincarnation. Like the birth of my child in a world so cold. Another living soul from the two love stole. A continuation of me from a seed I sewed will now grow old until his own unfold.

Do you believe in reincarnation? I'm going to live forever…

Roses Are Blue

Why would I honestly feel this way
What on earth have I done
I never knew that today would bring
Me closer to wanting to run

Run far, far away from you
After one of the best days of my life
How special a day last Valentine's
To end up cut as deep as a knife

I said everything was fine with me
Or at least that's how I felt
I didn't realize how much I care for you
Or that your actions would make my heart melt

One day I wake up with you in my arms
The next you're with another
You may say that nothing happened
But somehow I'm less than your lover

I don't want to sound like I'm judging you
I know you need time to grow
I only wish my feelings were not this deep
And that it took this to know

Shut The Hell Up

Shut your mouth all the way up
I don't like the smell of your breath
You talk too much when it's none of your
business
shut the hell up

No one's listening to what you're saying
talking all the damn time
can't be quiet even for a minute
just shut the hell up

Can't tone you out 'cause you're so loud
getting on everybody's nerves
talking a lot but ain't saying shit
why don't you just shut the hell up

Hush, be quiet, be still, silence
zip it, don't talk, not a word, shhhhhhh
close your mouth, whatever
just shut the hell up

Skin I'm In

To hell with being approved. I'm tired
of being used. I'm tired of being abused.
I'm tired of being ruled. I'm tired of being
schooled. If my TV works I'm on the news
and if I'm not being screwed, I'm still goin'
lose. I never got one acre and ain't seen no
damn mule.

I'm tired of being tired. They tell me to apply,
but I still don't get hired. My dark skin they
admire but they keep me under fire and
when it gets down to the wire, if I speak up
I'm a liar.

But what can I do, work a root like voodoo?
Is that what you do when you find yourself
in my shoes? Besides, who you, but me in
another nigga that's you?

Did you hear me, Black? Don't dwell on that.
Life's all out of whack. If they had their way
I'd stay on my back. They say learn how to
act and choose the right track, but every time
I'm down they're pushing me crack.

"Pull over nigger!" is what he said, but I'm
just hanging by a thread and even though
I fled, I didn't want to be dead. Now I'm
stopped by the Feds with a gun to my head
all because the light was red.

Somebody Black robbed the A&P, but even
though it wasn't me, no matter my plea…
guilty. To the first, second and third degree.
How in the hell can this be?
Is my dark skin the enemy? Fifteen years
'cause they envy me.

I ain't seen one yet, "To Serve and Protect."
But I damn sure bet they can't wait to get
a rope around my Black neck just to see a
brother sweat. But still I never will regret
being Black and being direct even with all
the hell I catch.

I'm living in sin from the skin I'm in, but I've
got to find a way to win from within. We're
treated like boys, but dammit we're men
swinging in the wind again and again never
knowing when this life will end.

Getting guns for protection just because of
my complexion, but what I need is some
direction of how to get a resurrection that
will free me their obsession with my skin.

Skin Tones

Are you Black and proud
Or just Black and loud
Does the earth tremble from the smell of
your feet
Were you always this dark
Or is that just a mark
From where your mom didn't watch what to
eat

Why the stare
That ain't your real hair
I bet it's (snap) that short and (snap) that
nappy
At least I do
have a good grade or two
Along with dimples from my pappy

Shhhhhhhh…listen, you hear that?

Don't whisper light, bright,
And damn near white
You ain't no bed of roses yourself
Uppity ass
Like you got class
Yellow is not a sign of good health

You ain't all that
In fact you're fat
Thinking you're gonna rain on this parade
You need to let go
Looking like a ho
Always looking for a brother that's paid

Shhhhhhhh…wait, you feel it?
Shhhhhhhhhh!

storm clouds

a whisper in the wind
silently saying good-bye
a listener feeling the breeze
looks up into the sky

now shivering at the thought
of his sunshine soon to end
praying the storm will pass
although not knowing when

the storm now drawing closer
the clouds begin to rise
the warmth of brightness fades
and darker become the skies

he quickly tries to escape
the softness of her voice
but the current getting stronger
does so without a choice

caught up in bad weather
the listener alone now cries
a drop of sad rain falls
a tear from soft brown eyes

looking beyond the storm
to see another day
the sun again will shine
with a bright rainbow to stay

Seven

For you I spared no expense
Only to share a love so tense
I accepted your kids and called them my own
And though it was rough still I held on
I was there for you when you needed me
But you couldn't decide how you wanted to be
On your job with roses by limousine
I fell on my knees and offered a ring
Embarrassed you fled while everyone screamed
Publicly humiliated -not quite like I dreamed
Said you were not ready our love you debated
I said good-bye and although I hate it, I waited
Two years later, seven in all
I proposed again during the fall
Even though you said *yes* things got pretty bad
7 months married was all we had
Now separated we wait for this divorce
Because being together is no longer a choice

Time Out

One more lady
No, one more friend
How in the hell
Did this begin

It was in her eyes
I saw my chance
Never got past "buddy"
So no romance

Playing on my kindness
How far will I go
Sharing all that I am
Any luck? Hell no

She's very attractive
In fact she's fine
She doesn't feel the same
I'm wasting my time
Wake up, fool!

Time...

Make me yours today
and I'll make today forever.

Too Soon

Love is for those that dare to dream.
Those dreaming that one day they will find
happiness.
But those dreams are sometimes interrupted
by reality.
The reality that she doesn't love you anymore
while wondering if she ever did.

So there you find yourself all alone once again.
Still you go on seeking the love that's inside
her yet to be.
Only to find more shattered dreams and a
heart filled with mixed emotions -confusion,
grief, pain.
A pain that only time can heal.
And time goes by ...slowly.

Never thinking that this could happen to you
for you gave your all, your very best
and sometimes more than you had to give.
Only to find a world of loneliness and
resentment.

Now vowing to never turn back
you look on to find what tomorrow has in
store.
Realizing tomorrow never comes you're left
with emptiness.
The question "why?" fills your soul
for you knew this one would last forever.
But here you are alone again, too soon.

Trust Him

Trust in God in all you do
For He's the one who will pull you through
When others say no and settle for less
He's the one that will say yes

Be encouraged and strong 'cause God is near
There's no need to worry, or wonder, or fear
His love is comforting, kind, and great
And He's much too wise to make a mistake

God was there when you took your first step
God was there every night when you knelt
God saved you from things when there was
no way out
So now we praise Him and dance and shout

It's all in his plan of divine salvation
Adore Him and love Him with no hesitation
God's mercy and love you've already won
So your speedy recovery has already begun

Wish It Away

Who are you and who am I
What makes you think I can't get by
Without you in my life
As my lover as my wife

Before you came I did okay
And even with you still I pray
To be happy for some peace
Not what comes between your knees

I chose you and no one else
I can do bad all by myself
You're so pretty you're so grand
That attitude makes me choose my hand

Being with you I'm filled with doubt
I feel uneasy when we go out
Not ever knowing what you might say
Hoping the evils in you will stay

Where they are quiet and cool
Or else you're going to act a fool
That is really what gives me stress
Ugly acts and ghetto mess

I can't live my life like this
I closed my eyes and made a wish
Try being kind when you're with me
Or turn me loose and let me be

Wait For Love

Some folks rush to be in love
they want it all and right now
when it ends they wonder why
when they should be wondering how

Some folks move too fast to love
for being in love is a thrill
but a hasteful love is a wasteful love
that may never be one that's real

Take your time and wait for love
it will come swift and strong
Then you will feel a powerful love
a love that can't go wrong

A real love can never die
it goes on as does life
it's the kind of love that changes us
turning a woman into a wife

Yes wait for love and you will see
it will be better in the end
For not only will you have your spouse to love
you will also have a friend

Oh Say Can You See

See you not the mess you've made
Lives ruined and for what
See you not a love betrayed
By irrational behavior of such

See you not the pain you've caused
Trying to let go but can't
See you not a world has paused
A torn heart in need of an implant

See you not this day would come
The truth you'd have to face
See you not just getting some
Would lead you to this place

See you not what's still inside
A calm of understanding
See you not the nights I cried
A precious time lost expanding

See you not the man I am
Is the man I've always been
See you not this little scam
Would bring us to this end

Why Are You Here

I'm a believer
All things happen for a reason
My world continues to crumble
Like the leaves this time of season

Who sent you here
I really thought I was coping
A twinkling eye, a pleasant smile
Sunshine was all I was hoping

If you came here
To tear a hole in my side
You may want to take a number
My wounds are deep and wide

What do you want
What else can I give
I know you're only passing through
So why can't I just live

What is my place
How do I fit in yours
Are my feelings too much for you
Am I only special behind closed doors

Why are you here
What is your divine plan
Was I only to be a stepping-stone
Or was there a chance at being your man

Why You

What makes you so good?
What makes you so sweet?
Why am I so excited every time we meet?
What makes you so perfect?
What makes you so right?
Why am I so mesmerized when you're in my
sight?
What makes you the one?
What makes you so grand?
Why am I so nervous when I touch your hand?
What makes you so worthy?
What makes you so smart?
Why am I so empty every time we part?
What makes you my world?
What makes you my choice?
Why am I so shaken up by hearing your voice?
What makes you all that?
What makes you so hot?

Why am I so into you even when you're not?
What makes you so wanted?
What makes you so true?
Why am I so much a fool when it comes to
you?

Your Move

The wrong moves at the wrong time
seems to be my story
I talk, I touch, I look for a way
to finally win back my glory

The wrong moves at the wrong time
as I write a new beginning
I ask, I listen, I wait for the sign
that lets me know I am winning

The wrong moves at the wrong time
this chapter reads much better
instead of blurting my feelings out
I start by writing a letter

The wrong moves at the wrong time
page after page I turn
I try, I fail, I pay the price
of a familiar lesson to learn

The wrong moves at the wrong time
the autograph signed in tears
I hope, I pray, I wonder if ever
looking back on all the years

The wrong moves at the wrong time
same cover, but different book
you may think you've read this one before
but take a closer look

Zero Degrees

Relationships come with gloomy days
sometimes ending with pain
leaving you broken, bitter, and torn
with nothing, it seems, to gain

So you start another relationship
with someone you find sincere
believing with all your heart and soul
this one will always be near

This one too, walks out of your life
you cry without an end
deciding that you have had enough
you harden instead of mend

You don't have time for those who ask
no matter the comfort they bring
for in your mind you believe it's true
they only want one thing

At times you try to be polite
but you're reminded of the past
then the temperature drops to zero
and the kindness does not last

It's very hard to earn your trust
so others keep feeling the breeze
of the cold hearted person you've become
as cold as zero degrees

Value Of A Wife

Every woman dreams of being a bride
To love, honor and cherish
Such a beautiful sound like ooh and ahh
With dreams of joy to flourish

A wife can be a very good thing
A welcomed distraction from the past
But one lacking emotion, support, or trust
Makes a togetherness that can not last

Saying "I do" does not make a wife
It only makes a bride
The fulfillment she brings into your life
An addition that gives you pride

Respect, commitment, companionship
Should be key to something real
Don't discount an old-fashioned woman
That cleans and cooks a good meal

Too many women today don't get it
Expecting to get a free pass
Out of all others he chose you to wed
To enhance the life he has

If he's good to you and your family
Then you probably found a good thing
It's expected that you would be the same
Even before you accept the ring

What will you offer to your marriage
A home of love and understanding
Or will you choose to break his spirit
With lots of constant demanding

A wife contributes more than sex
For their union is not of lust
Close your legs and open your mind
To the idea of love and trust

Trust that your man will be there for you
To provide and weather the storm
Believe in him to strengthen him
This too keeps his heart warm

Maintain the home as a peaceful place
Leave the world's troubles outside
Friendship, honesty, encouragement
Eliminates the thought to divide

Embrace your vows and hold on tight
you wont agree on everything
but as long as you put your husband first
He will honor his place as King

Open

You're taking a risk
You're taking a chance
You've dipped and kissed her
Without even a first dance

You're thinking too much
It's driving you crazy
You once could see clearly
But now it's all hazy

You're moving too fast
You were taking a break
Your being so into this girl
Could be a big mistake

You know too much
Your trust is limited
She tells you she loves you
But you know it's inhibited

You've been through so much
Why deal with this
She will only captivate your soul
To leave you in total bliss

You're a sucker for beauty
You've welcomed in pain
You've traded in your sunny days
For one that's filled with rain

You're so into her every way
Things are good, it seems
You're gonna wake up dying soon
'cause you're living a dream

Sit Still

Constantly moving, constantly looking
For the woman who will complete me
Constantly searching, never finding
Only accepting what I see

Constantly praying, constantly waiting
For a change in my life that's real
Constantly thinking, never believing
So I continue spinning the wheel

Undying Love

I'm asking you to sit and dare not speak
Cause your words somehow will make me
weak
I've held in so much for far too long
I pray my delivery does not go wrong
The trouble you may hear in the sound of my
voice
Is only due to this unforeseen choice
Hear me well for I must say
A lifetime of thoughts in just one day
I feel for you too strong for words
But knowing not of you is for the birds
My eyes get filled just from the thought
Of missing the love you've always fought
I tried to show you something more
A hole in my soul is what you tore
I remember you each night as I kneel
Praying my bleeding heart someday will
heal
How much is a person supposed to take
I never asked for anything fake
I don't deserve to be treated so cold
Because you waited for my past to unfold
My feelings for you are unimaginable
Simply pure and un-intangible
What I feel is unconditional

My daily routine is almost ritual
you've done nothing but push and shove
but I keep coming with undying love

Empty

Am I dead or am I dying
I'm getting frustrated from always trying
Stop deceiving, stop the lying
Why this bullshit I keep buying

It's all my fault, I'm to blame
Somehow I get caught up in this game
What's wanted from me is not the same
So again I find myself going insane

I found an angel, will she free me
Or will she too decide to flee
I can't be sure of what will be
I keep going farther than I can see

What's happening , I'm out of control
There's an emptiness in my soul
I never thought I fit the mold
But still for me the world seems cold

A walking zombie, that's what I am
Why do I even give a damn
An opened door means another slam
So what's the use I should just scram

Yeah scram and never look back
The odds of winning is quite a stack
Why run the race without a track
I must get out before I crack

Beyond My Grasp

Three times I reached out to comfort you
Each time you pulled away
I said I love you to show that I'm here for you
At any time throughout your day

I asked what was wrong because I care for you
To allow you to open your heart
Listening for as much or little as you wanted
to say
Was my way of allowing you to start

You spoke of your thoughts and nothing more
No explanations did you provide
Silently I continued to listen
Praying in me you'd confide

No spoken word followed my prayer
How much more could I have done
I offered myself in many ways
Receiving a partial response to only one

I'm not one to pressure you
These things only heal with time
I would hope to become everything to you
My passion for you will outgrow this crime

I will be here longer than always
To help close the door to this past
But you must find a way to believe in me
And not keep this thing beyond my grasp

Nowhere Fast

(A response to Running Shoes)
Stop making up these lies
And look at life as it is
I never asked you for a damn thing
So start off on the real

You saw my life from the beginning
Nothing hidden and no secrets
You knew I was a married man
But you chose to look past it

Now you want to be a victim
Want to cry over spilled milk
I'm the fool that allowed you in
And now you want to trip

I'm here daily just for you
But running scared is what you see
I'm the only man you've ever known
Then again you don't know me

You're always looking past what's here
Like these niggas want you for life
Always wanting to venture out
While wondering if I might

I'm the one who's stable, dear
I'm the one who cares
But for some reason unknown to me
You see me as your spare

You talk about my marriage
As if you know anything at all
Nothing is perfect the first time around
Not even with you, baby doll

How dare you come at me with this view
You better think about what you're saying
I'm not some nigga to push around
Like those idiots in your clan

<u>You</u> decided to get with me
All of your own free will
So don't act like you're stuck in this
You can leave whenever you feel

Don't mistake my kindness for weakness
I've done far more for you than anyone
Instead of respecting what we could be
You rather kill us with your tongue

I   Am   A   Man
I will not apologize for that
It's not my fault you've never seen one
Seems all I've heard about was trash

You say I don't talk to you, I run
You know damn well that's a lie
I'm always the one trying to talk it over with you
While your nose is in the sky

"I don't want to talk about it"
You say when confronted with the truth
Constantly blaming me for your faults
And who bought you those damn shoes

You really know how to piss me off
It's a good thing you know how to write
Because you're never woman enough face to face
With nerve enough to start this fight

You damn right I didn't open the door
I let you stand out there like a fool
Now you see how you treat me
Mean, evil, and down right rude

You said you stayed home to be with me
Funny how I couldn't tell
I didn't leave until 9pm
Same time you would have returned from there

I was ignored from the moment you arrived
You even asked if I was bored
None-the-less no time for me
So I decided to floor it

And to show how much you mean to me
I left because you asked about dinner
Seemed you were not cooking and neither
was I
So I went out thinking "I'll win her"

But you're so stubborn you can't see
I didn't get any for myself
You never broke away from the comfort I provide
So again I waited to death

You really feel that my life is a mess
Because of my running away
I know when it's time to separate myself
Like when ignored by you, okay

Why should I stay building frustration
Only to satisfy you
If you were here for me, why not be with me
Instead of emailing the crew

Don't ever think without you I'd die
You don't even understand who I am
Think next time before you write
And don't forget whose door you slam

That's right I state what's mine and what's yours
That is the way it is with you
I've done everything to show you that I want
us to be together
And you're talking about some damn
running shoes

You act as if your memory is lost
Thinking I get jealous over your guys
Jealousy is not the problem here
It's your bullshit games and lies

Lady I opened my home to you
I also opened my heart
So because I don't wait for you to decide to
spend time with me
You think I'm breaking this apart

No, my dear, its all you
With your attitude and your irresistible
sashaying
Can't wait for every nigga in a room to notice
you
Like I'm a fucking game you're playing

I told you before this got started
What I wanted in a woman
I must come first as I placed you
But very last is where I come in

I told you I like attention
You said you're not affectionate
I watch you when we're out on the town
I have to remind you that it's me you're with

Nice try with your little poetic gesture
To show your boiling anger
But I've been nothing but loving to you
And you've proven to be nothing but danger

You talk about how much you take
Let's hear about what you've given
Sex can be bought and paid for
And anyone can be a live-in

What's the use in loving you
When you have no love to share
It's really a shame, I am to blame
My love only gets me nowhere

At What Cost

Too many times it's been said
That we men don't use our heads
So sometime things fall apart
I guess it's because we use our hearts

Too many women have said good-bye
Most of them not understanding why
They felt the love inside was gone
I never convinced them they were wrong

Now here I am again, today
Wondering if this one will stay
But trouble for us is on the rise
How much should I compromise

I've given my all now I'm tapped out
Trying to show her what I'm about
Questioning what should be understood
Constantly attacking my manhood

Confusion is brought on by the least of things
And although she's my queen, I must be King
As much as I try to meet her demands
She's still unclear of where I stand

So the drama continues igniting the fire
Of unwritten rules to meet her desires
Like a butterfly she must be free
But why should her freedom cost me me

Off Track

I started out in the hole
I'm still in the hole
Trying to get back on my feet
One spouse behind
But still I'm blind
A woman that smelled so sweet

I didn't really know her
But wanted to show her
A love that could be so true
I churched out my pockets
Pawned even my sockets
And borrowed from others too

What was I doing
What am I always doing
Getting deeper and deeper into debt
I had to do it
Didn't care who knew it
I ain't figured the total yet

This was a new year
It was supposed to be *my* year
Everything done was to benefit me
But somehow I lost it
My plan I tossed it
For a skirt raised well above the knee

Muddy Waters

I stood at the alter confessing my love
For all the world to see
I pledged a ring to a sweet young thing
I really believed I was happy

Now I had what I've always wanted
A family to call my own
But it didn't last, it was over too fast
And all my happy was gone

I began dating a woman I knew
Who quickly brought back the smiles
No time to heal, this one was real
With her I traveled for miles

Discomfort began to settle in
She didn't want me like I thought
It was only physical, made me feel miserable
Instant comfort was what I sought

Back to my spouse I found myself crawling
With emptiness all around
Now in comes a baby, mine maybe
As my world was tumbling down

Back on my own I met someone else
That made me feel alive
I started the chase as she picked up the pace
Sending me for a nose dive

Another child was what she gave
Another baby girl
Without a blink and no time to think
Engulfed by this new world

Nothing went the way I planned
Seems I was in a mess
A lesson to learn, no where to turn
I must do what's best

I have to make the most of my new life
Provide for my two daughters
The new me begin where the old me ends
Drifting in muddy waters

Bookey

When you came in my life
I was just a kid
Barely knew right from wrong
Couldn't see
That the things you did
Would later make me strong

I hated you
When you said no
And I didn't get my way
I cursed your name
With every blow
As my sore behind hit the hay

I never believed
You were sincere
Said you were only being mean
But you stuck around
Year after year
Making sure we lived life clean

You made me study
You pushed me hard
Wanting me to make the grade
Now looking back
I thank God
For the wonderful man he made

From the Cub Scouts
To the Boys Club
It was you who was always there
Whether parade days
Or little league scrub
You were the man to care

When I came of age
I wanted a job
No more asking for your money
You wouldn't allow it
Felt you were a snob
Looking back it all seems funny

You always wanted
me to excel
A job would affect my scores
I stayed in my books
No need to rebel
Just studied and did chores

I finally left home
Going away to school
To do as I was allowed
All grown up
But free to be a fool
I wanted to make you proud

I never told you
In my own words
How much you mean to me
Men showing emotions
Is for the birds
But you know you're my Bookey

I do appreciate you
And all you've done
You could have walked away any time
A woman with three kids
Many men would have run
Such a great big mountain to climb

No better man
Could have been my father
I'm very proud you're in my life
After giving me birth
Mom's ex didn't bother
And you made her a very blessed wife

I'd like to think
I would do the same thing
I'm strong enough to carry the load too
I even tried
When I vowed with a ring
Now I take my hat off to you

You've touched my life
So many times
Just by being yourself
If saying I love you
Compares to crimes
Hide this evidence on the bookshelf

I Love You, Daddy.

We Got Next

Your life could end just as it began
With no conscious control of yourself
But who wants to think of getting older
While still in perfect health

Take just a moment to look at your life
Think of the days to come
Look at the seniors in your family
We all surely have some

Life brings changes everyday
Some say we live and learn
We go through life in similar ways
And we each will get our turn

Some days are great and happy and clear
Filled with high hopes of spirit and song
But days of blurs in our memory
Will also come along

We're so content being who we are
Taking our "todays" for granted
We never think that come tomorrow
Our straight and narrow may be slanted

We act as if we will never change
Intact our minds and bodies will remain
But look ahead to a generation of seniors
I wonder if they believed the same

Sure we're sad when we look at our elders
Our hearts go out to them
But one day not long we'll walk the same path
If we're lucky to keep each limb

What will you do when your turn come
How do you want to be cared for
When your macho-man/independent woman
days are gone
Who will you say you were there for

Will your family support you during your time
With visits and calls by phone
Or will you receive what your elders get
A dreaded cold life alone

Under Attack – Attack Back

Other man to the brother man
Puts crack on Black
Which makes Black on Black
Why can't you see that
Regroup, attack

Don't settle for can't
When you can my man
Thinking you've got the plan
In the palm of your hand
Get rid of that crack
Regroup, attack

Yo brother man in your brand new suit
Think you're part of a troop
A token flying the coop
Need to check out your roots
Before you shoot
You know better than that
Regroup, attack

New generation
Since emancipation
Think about the relation
You were kings of a nation
Don't settle for that
Regroup, attack

Make haste, embrace
And pick up the pace
No time to waste
Stand face to face
To claim your place
Be proud to be Black
Regroup, attack

Mood Swings

Are you happy or are you blue
Sometimes it's hard to tell with you

Are you up or are you down
Is your smile simply hiding your frown

One minute you like me the next you don't
Do you know what it is you want

Are you angry or just your tone
Or do you really want me gone

You say you care but I don't know
Maybe it's time for me to go

You're constantly going through many things
Or it just your mood swings

When You Cry

When you cry is it for me
Are you missing the love I gave
So filled with hope
Our inseparable union
Is it so torn we cannot save

When you cry is it for you
Are my mistakes too much to bear
Engulfed by your past
Entrapped with pain
Are we worth enough to even care

When you cry is it for now
Are you willing to grow with me
The sadness you feel
Will pass in time
Only if you allow your heart to see

When you cry is it for us
What did "we" really mean to you
Ever since we met
Love held my heart
Did you ever truly love me too

When you cry is it for life
Will I love you for the rest of my years
Our beautiful child
A reflection of us
Are you crying to heal or just for tears

She Loves Me

Is this love that she feels
Or could it just be excitement
That makes her speak of me so frequently
Ever since our first night spent

Are these feelings inside of me
From a true love that I've earned
Could her smile be as genuine as her
heartbeat
Or is her loving ways something she learned

Has all the love I've shown to her
Closed my mind at the thought
That maybe after all I've done for love
It is still something she fought

Could the love I feel she has for me
Come only from my need
Of wanting so much for her to want me
That I'm willing to let my heart bleed

Is this the love I dreamed about
One-sided and intense
Or does she really truly love me
And my questions are just nonsense

Never Forget

From a land to a ship
Through the sand by a whip
I'll remember

From a time that stood still
In a line against my will
I'll remember

From a Man to a boy
In a land with no joy
I'll remember

From being allowed to treated cold
In a crowd to be sold
I'll remember

From a place not forgotten
To a race picking cotton
I'll remember

From being free with great hope
To a tree by a rope
I'll remember

From a King to a slave
Voices ringing from the grave
I'll remember
       …lift every voice

A Husband's Prayer

Hear my prayer Oh Lord this day
Is there a lesson in living this way
I tried being humble and letting go
With tears of life my heart did show

How can I turn this thing around
True love I wanted but was not found
Our happiness ended far too soon
Diminished just after the honeymoon

Insecurity didn't just creep in
It never left since way back then
Can it be possible for love to succeed
Getting drunk and smoking weed

What would keep her out all night
Not coming in til broad daylight
Another man as I was told
When I ask the room turns cold

Her actions show she can't be trusted
I didn't stop til she was busted
Showing no respect for me, her spouse
Calling him while I'm in the house

I guess she never knew I knew
Her actions told me we were through
Now Lord I'm here, how can this be
She never really wanted me

My feelings for her are not the same
They changed before I knew his name
To live with him would he concur
He wouldn't even acknowledge her

Is it too late to ease the pain
To stop the noise that brings the rain
Help me escape this dream I live
Allow my heart to soon forgive

Forgive me for the choice I made
An insane home the price I paid
Now clear my mind as we depart
And give us both a brand new start

Girl School

Is it just my imagination
Or do all girls go without hesitation
To a place that provides summation
For almost any and every situation

And is it true that what they hear
Can be passed on the following year
To the next in line to lend an ear
For advice on matters held as dear

If we men are around enough
We will surely hear the same old stuff
Almost verbatim whether sweet or rough
And if not careful it could get tough

It seems almost like deja vu
It's a repeat of what we've been through
And even if they were right there too
Their time will come and they will do

Just what they've learned while in class
Whether to smile and let it pass
Or really act just like an ass
Either way you're lower than grass

Watch yourself while trying to be cool
Any man can be a fool
By not being cautious of this rule
Every woman goes to girl school

Sincerity

You ask how can I be real
When realness is all I can offer
As a man I must be harder
But your love makes me much softer

You ask how can I be trusted
When trust is what brought us together
I admit I've caused this heartache
But I intend to see you better

You ask how can I be sure
When surely I've always known
The feelings suppressed inside of me
Have now become full blown

You ask how can I love you
When loving you is where I began
From the moment I first laid eyes on you
To falling asleep hand in hand

You ask how can I see forever
When forever my love will last
My life without you is just a dream
Of our beautiful future that passed

You ask how can I be sincere
When sincerely I'll share my life
With you and only you
If you would be my wife

Captivity

It was in cool November
The day we met
Her eyes meeting mine
I'll never forget

She was so beautiful
I could not refrain
Asking my dear friend
For my new friend's name

In a slammin' suit
Of fuchsia and gray
She simply smiled
And responded with "hey"

We spoke as if
We shared a past
Her lovely features
Made my heart beat fast

I often visited her
From day to day
Her warmth was so special
I could not stay away

We worked at the same place
Only separated by fixtures
And even though she had a man
She posted my pictures

I was intrigued
It caught me by surprise
I knew we were only friends
But that was a disguise

Deep down I already knew
She was what I wanted
Like a reoccurring dream
My mind became taunted

We saw each other by day
At night we spoke by phone
Captured by her sensuality
I prayed nothing went wrong

The chemistry was magical
Our families intertwined
It appears there was a history
Between her folks and mine

She moved in as a roommate
And later became much more
The Super Bowl played in my room
But no one was keeping score

We grew closer falling in love
A cute family we soon started
Now all of my lonely days
Have since then departed

What's In A Name

I never imagined true love could fail
An event that only time would tell
You knowing all along we were done
With every breath I gave to you
Seems caring was one thing I could do
Always hoping I was the one
Trying to avoid this situation
Letting go was my contemplation
Even though it wasn't my decision
Voodoo must have been my curse
I felt that nothing could be worse
Needing to be right with such precision
I needed to believe it was not me
A perfect us just could not be
To even think it was a lie
You loving me was a line you ran
Your love for me with another man
While aimlessly he made you cry
Useless memories broke the cocoon
With another baby in your womb
And no father to pretend it's his
To dazzle me you set out to do
Cause he would have no part of you
Just what do you think this is
In the end the truth came out
Showing me what you're about

Deceit and dishonest distaste
For within a name without a clue
You chose a man that didn't choose you
Making my dreams with you a waste

Old Like New

Some things never change
Only repeats itself in a new beginning
The old you is still the same
And my head is no longer spinning

Confused I was yesterday
Thinking we were inseparable
You came back just to say
The damage is past irreparable

Must there be a way to turn this around
Many said to let it go
Where is the love in you I found
And why does it continue to grow

Every step forward I look two steps back
Together what we shared felt so real
A rebuilt love is not the same stack
But my love is beyond my will

Intangibles

The union of man with woman just one
Has always been a source of magic
But sometimes life's cruelties
Will prove our actions as tragic

There must be a way to make this right
A way to take away this sorrow
Knowing today brings a new hope
Although unsure about tomorrow

Imagine a world where love is true
One with no ups and downs
A place where love grows higher
With no limits or outer bounds

Bring on the warmth that gives us life
That sunshine after the rain
In the face of reason give me a sign
A contemplation of glory regained

Meant To Love

I thought I could make you love me
If only I shared something real
I thought if I loved you enough
No other way could you feel

I thought if I offered you my life
You'd see how much I love you
Year after year I gave and waited
Seems I was practicing voodoo

I thought if I made your life easier
You would let go of the past
I thought my heart would shatter your pain
And you would open up to me at last

I thought being good would win you
I tried to restore your trust
You never let down your guard with me
I guess I never got past lust

I thought honesty would soften your heart
Allowing real love to get inside
Constantly fighting with you to be with you
Though broken and torn I tried

I thought I could be your forever
If only you would let me
I wanted you to want me too
And never ever regret me

I thought I could make you see my fire
My feelings go beyond and above
I thought you could be my everything
Maybe we were not meant to love

Unfavorable Differences

She placed me on a pedestal
Only to tear me down
A crown for a day until dismay
Then King begins to drown

I thought I knew what pleased her
Though we didn't always agree
Now that I could take, but for goodness sake
Where comes the need to degrade me

One minute I'm great and no one better
A man that lives for her
Until the time the good rewinds
Then I become some other

I never know what to expect
She's happy or evil or sad
Then I change to rearrange
Still unable to combat what's bad

Unlocking the essence of her highs
Ends always with more
If compatibility is the key
How can I find the right door

Righting Wrongs

Each day ends as it began
With you on my mind piercing my heart
Now facing the fear of life without you
I don't know where to start

I was too busy blaming you
For all the troubles that we shared
So filled with anger and discontentment
In your needs I never cared

Providing for us should be enough
The rest would fall into place
Foolish of me to have this notion
Leaving in you an empty space

I never thought I needed you
Though loving you was by day and night
Thinking I had it all figured out
Seems I was wrong trying to be right

Dance Fever

Late at night you're away from me
Going out to the club
If I could I would go along with you
But its not your average pub

Oh yeah there is a DJ
And yes you can even dance
But most that come for this party scene
Are waiting for their chance

Their turn to get up close and personal
While you dance to the beat
Big smiles assures they are pleased
While you shake shake shake your booty

I know that this is your job
And I'm not one to complain
But you feel that I should respect it
And lie about it just the same

My family shouldn't know what you do
But I'm supposed to be so proud
That I get the girl dancing for money
But dare not say it aloud

What's wrong with bumping and grinding
On a few strangers or old friends
Or exposing a piece of privacy
As long as they're dropping dividends

Who but pimps accept this life
You're gone more than half the night
Enough time to do only God knows what
While away and out of sight

You juggle the fantasy this fever brings
While trying to hold onto what's real
A man that cares so foolishly for you
He dismisses the way he feels

So dance angel of the night
They'll make it rain now and forever
Dance mommy get that paper
While a trustful relationship you sever

Dream Girl

Only in my dreams
Could I have found a love as this
An opened heart of passion
That began with just one kiss

Gazing in your eyes
I saw my heaven to hold
With immeasurable affection
A love not often told

A beauty from within
The magic of something new
So giving and understanding
Supportive and so true

A fairy tale of sorts
With real wonder it seems
The perfect girl for me
But only in my dreams

Obituaries

All around every age and sex
No need to guess who will be next
Just listen closely to the chit-chat
And you will hear exactly that
Whether a loud yell or just a squeak
Death comes from the words she speak
You may be safe but just for a while
Especially if she does not smile
She will cut you down to size
A killer you need to recognize
She does not care who she offends
Don't look to her to make amends
Cause you'll be dead right where you stand
Without so much as a lifted hand
Her nasty tongue and evil mind
Pushes a death that's mean and blind
So avoid your doom of verbal thirst
By sharpening your words to kill her first

Opposites Distract

I see you
Do you see me
Tell me how we are to be
Passers by whenever we meet
I nod you nod
That's how we greet

Lost in time
But I'm still here
Funny how I just want you near
By my side where I can feel
The love I seek from you at will

There you go
Doing your thang
Some call me ass say I'm a pain
I want you to have my name
But still I feel its just a game

I give in
While you give out
I try being calm but still I shout
To get my point expressed aloud
Just one on one without the crowd

Here we are
Going through life
Another girl but not a wife
I'm here for you both day and night
Trying till we get this right

You're from now
I'm from back when
Our differences wouldn't be the end
Now one event its to the wind
But forever for you I will send